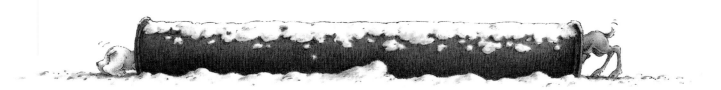

For Davy

First published in the United States, Great Britain, Canada, Australia, and New Zealand
in 2005 by North-South Books Inc., an imprint of NordSüd Verlag AG, Zürich, Switzerland.

First paperback edition published in 2007 by North-South Books Inc.
Distributed in the United States by North-South Books Inc., New York.

Library of Congress Cataloging-in-Publication Data is available.
A CIP catalogue record for this book is available from The British Library.

ISBN-13: 978-0-7358-2029-6 / ISBN-10: 0-7358-2029-5 (trade edition)
10 9 8 7 6 5 4 3 2
ISBN-13: 978-0-7358-2030-2 / ISBN-10: 0-7358-2030-9 (library edition)
10 9 8 7 6 5 4 3 2 1
ISBN- 13: 978-0-7358-2139-2 / ISBN-10: 0-7358-2139-9 (paperback edition)
10 9 8 7 6 5 4 3 2 1

Printed in Belgium

www.northsouth.com

Little Polar Bear
and the Reindeer

Written and Illustrated by

Hans de Beer

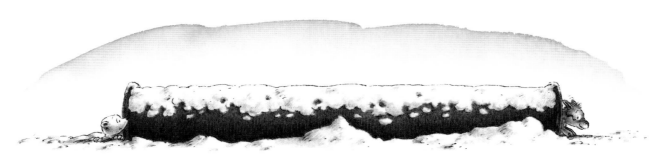

Translated by J. Alison James

NORTHSOUTH
BOOKS
New York / London

Lars, the Little Polar Bear, lived at the North Pole. There, among the ice and snow, he felt at home.

Most of the year, Lars's world was white with icy cold. For only a few months each summer, the ground warmed up. Fresh grass and plants grew, tempting the animals who for the rest of the year lived farther south.

One morning, Lars noticed a thin film of ice on the water. It was a sure sign that summer was over. The animals would now start their migration, as they did every year. Lars heard a chorus of honking geese and looked up. Huge flocks were already on their way to the warmer lands in the south.

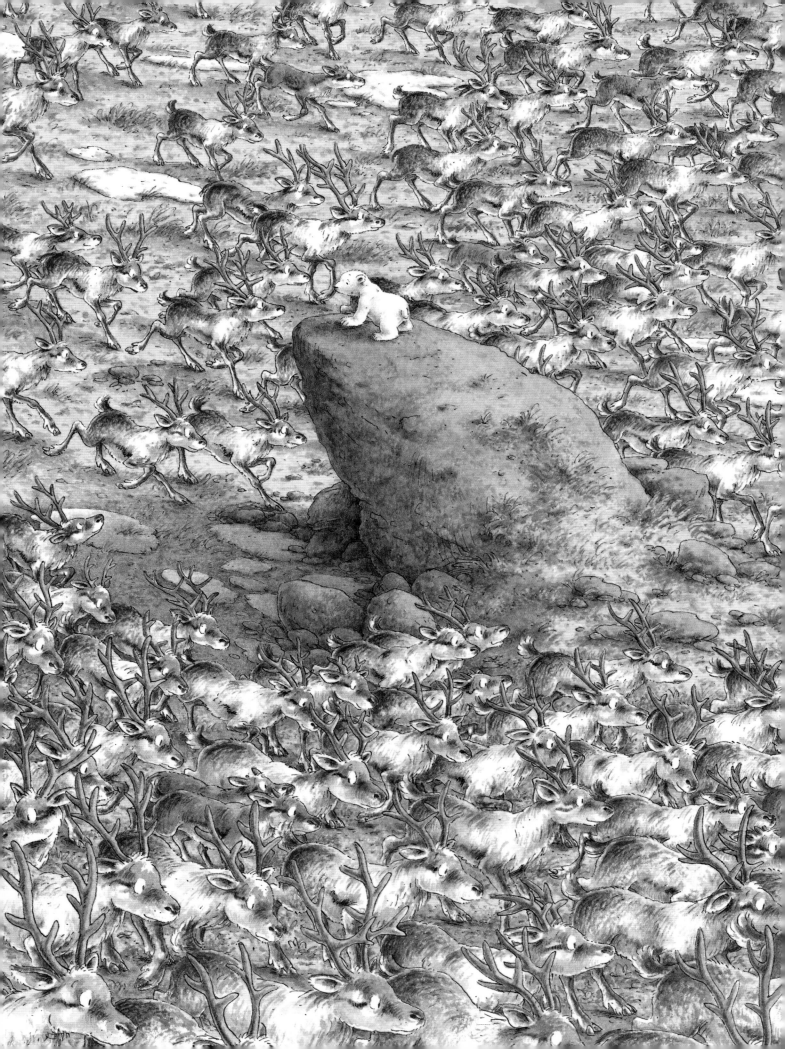

Lars felt the earth tremble beneath him. Were the reindeer on the move, too? He quickly scrambled up on his lookout rock—and just in time. The giant herd rushed past him, a pounding river of reindeer.

Right behind them, a huge snowstorm blew in. Thick flakes of snow swirled around Lars. He quickly ducked under a rocky ledge that protected him from the worst of the storm.

It stormed for hours. When it stopped, the arctic tundra lay under a thick cover of snow. Lars loved the first snow. He ran all around, delighted by the huge tracks his paws made.

Something moved in front of him. Suddenly an animal poked its head out of the snow.

"Oh!" said Lars, surprised.

"Oh!" cried the strange animal, frightened.

The Little Polar Bear blinked. "You're a little reindeer!" he said in a friendly voice. "I'm Lars, the Little Polar Bear. What's your name? And why are you here all alone under the snow?"

"I . . . I'm Oliver," stuttered the little reindeer. "I lost my mother in the storm. I know she is searching for me, but how will she ever find me? I'll never see her again!" he wailed.

"Don't worry, Oliver," comforted Lars. "Your mother must be waiting for you with the herd. I'll go with you, and together we can look for her. Just tell me what direction the herd went."

"That way, south," said Oliver.

After they had walked for a while, Lars asked nervously, "How do you reindeer know which direction south is?"

"I don't know," said Oliver. "We just do."

Lars and Oliver came to a river.

"We'll have to swim across," the Little Polar Bear explained.

"But I can't swim!" Oliver trembled at the sight of the water.

"Come on, Oliver. Swimming is easy." Lars went out into the water. "Come on. You'll see. You can do it."

And sure enough, Oliver *could* swim, even faster than Lars. Little Polar Bear laughed with relief.

Slowly it grew dark. Oliver anxiously looked out across the wide tundra. "My mother always warned me of dangerous wolves that hunt in the dark," he whispered.

"No problem when I'm around," boasted Lars. "Wolves are afraid of polar bears."

As night fell, they heard muffled heavy movements in the distance. The sounds came closer and closer, until they could see eyes glowing in the darkness. "D-d-don't be a-a-fraid, Oliver," stuttered Lars.

"No, don't be afraid, youngsters," growled a giant animal. It was Otto, the great musk ox, who stood before them. "Come, rest among us for the night."

"You see," Lars whispered a little later, "with me, you are safe from wolves."

But Oliver was already fast asleep.

The next day, Otto the musk ox and two of his friends offered to travel along with Lars and Oliver. "The herd can't be far," said Otto. "We just saw it yesterday."

The snow was too deep for Lars to move quickly on his short legs.

"Come, Little Polar Bear," said Otto with a laugh. "Climb on my back, or we'll never catch up with the reindeer!"

Soon they saw fresh reindeer tracks in the snow. Oliver ran over to them. "I'm coming. I'm coming, Mama!" he shouted happily.

There it was, the great herd of reindeer.

Oliver's mother ran to meet him. "Oliver, at last! I have been looking everywhere for you," she said. She thanked Lars and the musk oxen for their help. But she looked worried. "The migration has stopped. We can't go any farther," she said. "Come and see for yourselves."

The little group made their way to the front of the reindeer herd. A tall wire fence with wooden rails stretched across the tundra for as far as they could see. Behind the fence ran a thick pipeline.

Little Polar Bear saw a goose beyond the fence. "Hey, goose," he said, "is there an opening in this fence somewhere?"

"No, the fence is endless," the goose replied. "And in the places where the pipeline is not yet built, there are huge piles of pipe."

Lars listened thoughtfully.

"Come on!" called Little Polar Bear. "Let's see where the pipe is stacked."

Lars studied the piles. Then he had an idea. "Oliver, bring the herd here," he called. Little Polar Bear climbed over the fence, searching for something. Soon he came back with a thick cable.

Otto quickly understood what Lars was planning to do. "Great idea," he said.

Lars wrapped the cable around the lowest pipe. He looped the other end around the shoulders of the musk oxen, and they began to pull.

"Keep going!" Lars encouraged them. "Pull . . . and pull . . . and pull!"

Slowly, step by step, they moved forward.

Soon the pipe began to shift a little. Then all of a sudden, it pulled loose. The entire pile came crashing down with a deafening roar and broke through the fence.

Everything—pipe, fence, and rails—lay scattered on the ground.

"Onward reindeer! To the south!" cried Lars.

A relieved herd of reindeer headed through the gap.

"That was a fantastic idea," said Otto.

Oliver and his mother thanked Lars and the musk oxen, then bid them farewell.

The Little Polar Bear and the little reindeer were sad.

"Next summer, we'll see each other again," said Lars.

"Of course we will," agreed Oliver.

Lars watched the departing reindeer for a long time. He felt proud, and he was happy to see them head across the river toward the forest. But he already missed his new friend, Oliver.

The musk oxen accompanied Lars all the way back home. Overhead, a last flock of geese flew south.

"Bring greetings to my friend Oliver," called Lars. "And from Otto, too!" he shouted, laughing.